The Mussel Princess

The Mussel Princess
A fairy tale

from Willi Fritz and Evelyn Fritz
with illustrations by Lottie E. Hotaling

Bibliographical Information of the Deutsche Nationalbibliothek
This publication is listed in the Deutsche Nationalbibliographie of the
Deutsche Nationalbibliothek; detailed bibliographical information
can be accessed under http: //dnb.d-nb.de
© 2014
Translated from the original German by Marianna Kirchner
Printing, Production and Layout: BoD – Books on Demand
ISBN: 978-3-7357-1128-1

Many years ago in a big forest lived an evil witch, who was very ugly. She would turn all those who got lost in the forest into small objects.

Either she would turn people into a little stone, or a mushroom, or even into a pine cone.

When she could kick these little motionless objects along with her foot, she would chuckle for joy, and her witch's heart laughed.

This witch lived in a little wooden house. Her only servant was a raven, who was very devoted to her. From the highest perch he would keep a lookout to see if anyone dared to enter the forest.

If this occurred, he would fly quickly to the witch's house and report it to her, and she would

run out of the house and
look for the person to cast
a spell upon.

Not far from the forest,
a beautiful castle stood on a
mountain. There the king who
ruled the land lived together
with his wife, the queen, and
their daughter the princess.

The princess was pretty, had
learned her lessons diligently and
therefore also knew a lot. This
was known throughout the land.

Many a king's son had come to the castle for this reason, and wanted to take the princess as a wife.

This was not so easy, however, since the king had made a condition that a prince could only marry his daughter if he managed to outwit the evil

witch in the forest and do away
with her.

But all the suitors hesitated; although they would have liked to take the princess as a wife, none had dared to do battle with the witch. And so they had to return alone to their own country.

Thus the time passed, and the princess complained to her father, the king, that she would never find a husband. But the king said: "Have patience, my little daughter, someday one will come who also has great courage".

And the king was right. One beautiful summer day a brave prince came to the castle, and since he loved the princess at first sight, he accepted without hesitation the difficult condition the king made, to do battle with the witch.

But the princess, who had also liked the prince immediately, did not wish him to go alone. So she begged her father to let her go with him. The king replied: "If you promise me that you will not enter the forest, but will wait outside until the prince has conquered the evil witch, then you can go".

The princess promised, and both went together towards the forest. The prince was looking forward to meeting the witch, but he was unaware of what powers of bewitchment she possessed, against which he was helpless. And so he chatted merrily about his homeland.

The princess enjoyed listening to him. Then they reached the outskirts of the forest, and the princess now waited as her father had wished.

The prince departed with these words: "I will return soon, and then you will become my queen and surely be very happy with me". Then bravely he strode into the deep forest. The raven upon the high pine tree, however, had been observing the royal children for a long time already.

He flew down onto the witch's shoulder and reported everything to her. The witch chuckled: "What, the prince thinks he's stronger and can conquer me? Just you wait;

you'll get to know my might".
Then she sneaked towards the prince.

The prince, who saw the witch approach, asked: "Oh old woman, can you tell me where I can find the evil witch, or maybe you are her yourself?"

Just to be on the safe side, he withdrew his sword and prepared to do battle.

But the witch merely touched him and suddenly he could no longer move or speak. But he could still see and hear all what went on around him. So first he had to stand a very long time, because the witch disappeared.

She waited for the princess, so she could enjoy the full power of her witchcraft.

The princess had been waiting patiently up until now. But then she became fearful that something had happened to her prince. She forgot the words of her father and entered the forest.

This was just what the witch was waiting for! She went to meet the princess, and as the princess saw the ugly old woman, she became afraid and remembered what she had promised her father.

Still, she gathered up all her courage and asked the witch: "Oh dear old woman, have you seen my prince?" "Indeed I did see him", replied the witch, "he wanted to drive me out or even do away with me, hey? Ha ha ha. I know very well that your parents don't like me, and for this they will be punished, in that I cast a spell on you. The prince can return and tell it to your parents".

Then she led the young girl
to the place where the prince
still stood motionless, quickly
removed two halves of a mussel
shell, and spoke to the princess:
"You shall become so tiny that
you fit inside this mussel, and
my raven shall carry you off and
drop you into the ocean".

And so it happened that just in that moment, the princess was suddenly turned into a tiny wax doll and was placed by the witch inside the mussel. Then she tied a ribbon around it, and the raven flew off with the mussel.

Tears welled up in the eyes of the prince, who had to watch as this all happened. The witch touched him, so that he was able to move again. But she had taken his sword from him, so that he was powerless. The witch chuckled and said: "Go now, search for your princess and tell the king that the witch is really stronger than any king". And then she disappeared inside her little house.

31

The poor prince had no choice but to go back to the king and queen and report what had happened. And so he returned to the castle and told them everything. They were all very sad and wept for days on end.

Then the prince spoke: "I will build me a ship and sail the seas so long, until I find the princess in the mussel. And then I will go back to the witch and demand that the spell be broken".

The king did not believe that the prince would find the tiny floating mussel shell in the great wide ocean. But he didn't know what else could be done, and so he gave his blessings.

The prince had a good solid ship built, and he sailed for a long time across many seas, but there was no sign of the mussel.

He was about to give up, but then he thought of the poor princess who had to float on the sea forever, and so he continued to search. In the meantime it had become autumn.

On one quiet evening, the prince sat out on the deck and stared at the water for a long time. Since there was no wind, he couldn't sail further at that time.

Suddenly he saw many mermaids close by. He could hardly believe his eyes, as he saw one especially pretty mermaid playing with a mussel and tossing it about. Because this mussel was tied up with a bright ribbon, he thought, could this possibly be the one in which the bewitched princess was held?

This filled him with such joy that he sprang into the air, and made such a noise that the mermaid was startled and dived into the water, forgetting the mussel.

The prince then fished the mussel out of the water, untied the ribbon, and oh what joy, the bewitched princess lay within!

But how much greater was his happiness, as the tiny wax doll grew larger and larger, and suddenly the princess stood before him. Through his touch the spell was broken, because the old witch had in the meantime passed away.

The royal children were now so happy that they didn't notice how one mermaid kept swimming around the ship. She was searching for her plaything, and said to the prince: "I am the queen of the mermaids.
I believe that you have taken my favorite plaything, the mussel, away from me. If this is so, then please return my toy back to me".

He thought a moment, then as quickly as possible made a tiny doll that resembled the princess, put it inside the mussel, and tied a ribbon around it.

Then he gave the mussel to the mermaid with these words: "Here is your plaything again; it now looks exactly as it did before when you held it".

The mermaid was very pleased, spoke her gratitude, and disappeared again into the water.

The two royal children then sailed on home, and the parents in the castle cried for joy as they returned. Soon afterwards the wedding was celebrated and everyone was happy and content.

48

After a long time the mermaid queen became tired of her plaything, and one day she heedlessly tossed it onto a beach in the North Sea.

There the mussel lay for a long time, until one day a man walking along the beach found the mussel with the tiny doll inside.

He took it home and gave it to his daughter as a gift.

How the fairy tale originated:

Once on a beautiful day in the year 1951, a man took a walk along a beach in Buesum in northern Germany. While his thoughts wandered, his foot suddenly struck a mussel in the sand. He picked it up and while he looked at it, a story formed in his mind. He took the mussel back home and immediately wrote the story down on paper. Then he bought a tiny doll, placed it inside the mussel and tied a red ribbon around it. He sent the mussel to his daughter, who was with her mother on a visit to Hamburg.

About the book author, Willi Fritz, father of Evelyn Fritz:

Willi Fritz (June 21, 1923 – March 10, 1978) was born in Schlawe, Pomerania (now Poland). There he successfully completed education as a trained retail salesman. He was also head of a theatrical group. A few years after the end of the second World War, he took over a grocery store in Wesselburen (northern Germany). In 1962 he moved with his family to Groemitz, a Baltic Sea resort, where he worked as a self-employed businessman. From 1970 on he was an executive in the administrative authority of the health resort in Groemitz.

Willi Fritz and daughter Evelyn

About the artist,
Lottie Elizabeth Hotaling

Lottie Elizabeth Hotaling was born in Richmond, Virginia, USA.

Already at an early age she became interested in art, continuing a family tradition that goes back three generations with roots in Germany.

Lottie's mystical, fairylike figures are well known in juried shows in upstate New York (including Rhinebeck and Woodstock) where she lives with her family.

Lottie Hotaling also produces greeting cards and other imaginative art forms such as "knish art", as well as commissioned pieces. The gentle, dreamlike illustrations in The Mussel Princess are her first to be published in book form and are dedicated to her mother, Liselotte Gathmann Rieper, who has been her inspiration.